This book belongs to:

....

PARSON DIMLY'S TREASURE HUNT

Written & Illustrated by John Patience

DERRYDALE BOOKS
New York

Copyright © 1984 by Fern Hollow Productions Ltd
This 1984 edition is published by Derrydale Books,
distributed by Crown Publishers, Inc.
Printed in Italy
ISBN 0-517-445727

It was Sunday and Parson Dimly was busy in the church laying out the hymn books for the morning service. As he bustled around he sang to himself, "All things bright and beautiful." Suddenly another voice joined in.

"Chirp, chirp, chirp." The old mole looked up and saw a little sparrow. It had flown in through a large hole in the church roof.

"Good gracious," the parson exclaimed. "That hole must have been caused by the storm we had last night. I must get it fixed at once, but how on earth can I raise the funds?"

After giving the matter some thought, Parson Dimly decided to raise the money to mend the roof by holding a treasure hunt. The Fern Hollow animals all bought tickets and turned up with all kinds of vehicles. There were cars, motorcycles, a tandem, the fire engine and Sigmund Swamp on his bicycle. In fact, the only animal who arrived on foot was Polly Prickles. Poor Polly — no one thought she stood the slightest chance of winning the race to the treasure.

Now it was time to begin the treasure hunt by reading the first clue.

"Look in a tree, in a little round hole
which stands in a place by a happy old vole,"
read Parson Dimly.

Brock Gruffy realized at once what the clue referred to and quickly drove off to the Jolly Vole Hotel, where he jumped out of his car and ran down to the river bank to the hollow tree. Unfortunately, poor Brock forgot to put the car's handbrake on and his car rolled down the bank after him, and, with a great splash, ended up in the river!

The next animal to arrive at the hollow tree was
Sigmund Swamp. Sigmund read the clue —
Now you're wondering what to do
Where the river is crossed you'll find the next clue.
"That must mean Ferny Bank Ferry," said the clever
toad to himself, and away he went, pedaling furiously.

When Sigmund reached the ferry he rode out onto the
jetty to the signpost where he could see a piece of paper
had been pinned. Suddenly there was a loud bang and
Sigmund fell off his bicycle. The poor toad had ridden
over a nail and punctured a tire.

The clue pinned to the signpost at the Ferry read —
    The third clue you will find today
    Is where the farmer stores his hay.
It was easy to guess that this must mean Farmer Bramble's barn, and very soon the farm yard and the barn were crammed with traffic. Everyone had read the clue which was pinned to the barn door, but they had gotten themselves into such a jam that no one could get out!

Eventually Polly Prickles
arrived at the barn. She was
feeling rather tired because, of
course, she had had to run all
the way —
"To find the treasure run
as fast as you can,
Back to the place where
the hunt began,"
puffed Polly, reading the clue
on the barn door. Then away
she ran as fast as she could back
to the vicarage garden.

17

In the garden Polly found a huge hamper of food and a trophy with "Winner of the Grand Treasure Hunt" inscribed on it. Perhaps this wasn't real treasure, but it had all been great fun and Polly decided to share the hamper with all the other contestants and Parson Dimly, so they all had a lovely picnic.

The next day Parson Dimly counted the money that the treasure hunt had raised, and was pleased to find that it easily covered the cost of mending the church roof. Naturally, the work was done by Mr. Chips and his sons, Chucky and Flip, who did a very good job of it.

21

Fern Hollow

MR CHIPS'S HOUSE

MR WILLOWBANK'S COBBLERS SHOP

MR CROAKER'S WATERMILL

STRIPEY'S HOUSE

SCHOOL

THE JOLLY VOLE HOTEL

RIVER FERNY

MR ACORN'S BAKERY

MR RUSTY'S HOUSE

MR PRICKLES'S HOUSE

POST OFFICE

BORIS BLINKS'S BOOKSHOP

MR TWINKLE'S HOUSE

MR TUTTLEEBEE'S SHOP

MR THIMBLE'S TAILORS SHOP

WINDYWOOD